W9-BQY-664

DEC 0 8 2020

To my grandchildren, Felicity and Ciaran, facing the future.
And to my brother, Bernard, who had to face the future
and became my guiding shadow after our father died.

Phaidon Press Inc.
65 Bleecker Street
New York, NY 10012

Phaidon Press Limited
2 Cooperage Yard
London E15 2QR

phaidon.com

This edition © 2020 Phaidon Press Limited
First published in German as *Non Stop* by Diogenes
© 2019 Diogenes Verlag AG Zürich

ISBN 978 1 83866 159 5
004-0720

A CIP catalogue record for this book is available from the
British Library and the Library of Congress.

Printed in China

TOMI UNGERER

NON STOP

Edited by Aria Ungerer & Margaux de Weck

Birds, butterflies, and rats were gone.
Grass and leaves had withered.
Flowers had turned into memories.
Streets and buildings were deserted.
Everyone had gone to the moon.

Left behind,
Vasco roamed through barren solitudes,
following his shadow.

All at once,
it urged him to SCRAM around the corner.

JUST IN TIME!

Vasco rambled on,
humming and whistling.

His shadow directed him across the street.

JUST IN TIME!

Buildings toppled down,
like empty crates.

The shadow pointed to a wall ...

On the other side
crouched a creature called Nothing.

"Could you do something for me?" he asked.
"I have a letter here for my wife.
She has vanished."

"But there's no address!" said Vasco.
"It will find its way," murmured Nothing.

Vasco took the letter and left.

A tsunami turned the streets into rapids
of gushing, rushing water.
Vasco was deep in rising trouble —
he could neither swim nor float.

His trusted shadow
led him to a ladder.

JUST IN TIME!

Vasco climbed the ladder,
onto the deck of a ship.

The vessel was soon afloat,
steerless and adrift,
tossed about by angry surf.

After many long days, and longer nights,
it crashed upon shredding reefs.

With no lifeboat on board,
Vasco jumped into a barrel.

Vasco washed up on a beach,
and took shelter in a deserted hospital.

Through the wards,
the shadow led Vasco to two lonesome creatures.

Vasco handed over the letter from Nothing.
The creature read it with tears in her eyes.
"Please! Take my little Poco with you!" she implored.

Vasco clutched Poco to his heart.
At last he had someone to care for.

Just in time.

Overnight, the temperature dropped.
The ocean froze.

Vasco and Poco left the island,
tailing the shadow from floe to floe.

A heatwave followed close behind,
melting the ice at their heels.

When they reached solid ground,
on scorched soles,
Vasco followed his sizzling shadow
to the shade of branchless trees.

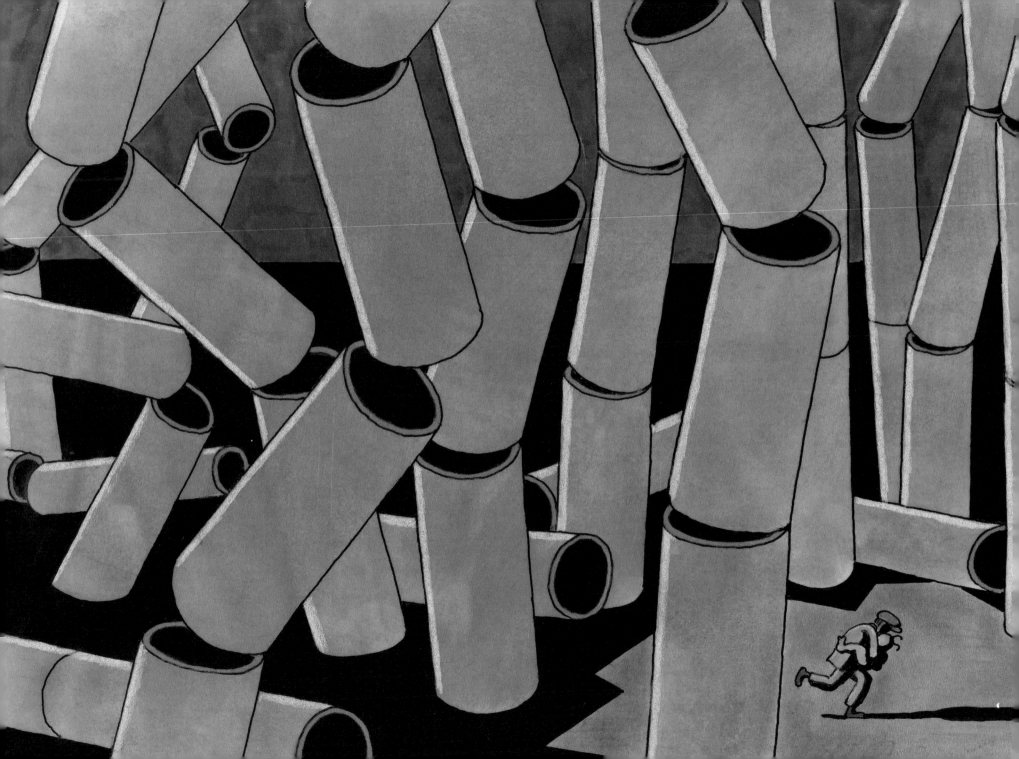

Tremors shook the ground.
The trunks began to rattle and tumble down.
The din was deafening ...

Pushing Poco ahead of him,
Vasco crawled through pipes and valves.

They emerged in the middle of an oil refinery.
Gas tanks were exploding,
disintegration seemed imminent.

Keeping doubt and fear at bay,
by focusing on Poco's sweet little face,
Vasco swerved between pits of gargling magma.

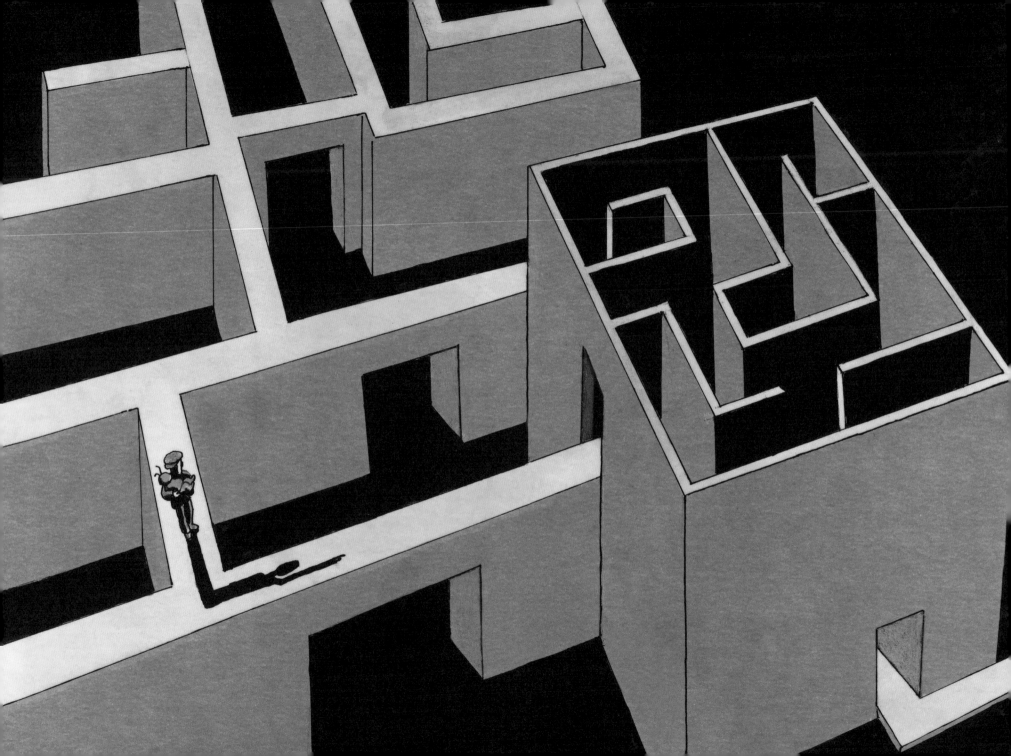

The bridge led to a maze,
but the shadow knew its way,
and guided the pair to the exit.

JUST IN TIME!

The buildings began melting
into globs of lilac gelatin.

Polluted by humanity,
the moon shone mottled black.
Down the road
the shadow hailed a taxi.

JUST IN TIME!

Driverless, the taxi took them to the middle of a city.

A pack of crushing Tiger tanks approached,
attracted by the boulevard's plastic trees —
their favorite food.

Hastened by the shadow,
Vasco and Poco took shelter in a metro station.

JUST IN TIME!

A train rolled in,
and came to a jagged halt.
Vasco and Poco embarked,
and the train left on time.

The train rambled for hours
in total darkness.
Vasco sang Poco lullabies
until both fell asleep.

They reached the end of the line,
and disembarked.
The train reversed
back where it came from.

The shadow aimed for the desert.

It was getting darker and the shadow dimmer.
Just in time,
Vasco looked up and saw in the distance
a phantasmagorical sight.

In the middle of the desert appeared
a gigantic cake covered in icing.
Steep, narrow steps
led to an entrance
between two maraschino cherries.

Inside were ample supplies of everything.

Alas!
In the softened light,
the shadow dissolved.
Having achieved its mission,
it vanished in silent modesty.

THE END ...

AFTERWORD

Sometimes, without his shadow,
Vasco felt sad and forlorn.
He often stepped outside,
into daylight,
to see his old friend again,
waiting for him,
like a faithful dog on the landing.

Poco remained small.
He learned to read,
turned into a scholar,
and a gifted, vegetarian pianist.

Vasco and Poco
were never bored.
To my knowledge, they are still aging there,
sheltered in peace.